Jeffrey and Sloth

Jeffrey and Sloth

Story by
Kari-Lynn Winters

Illustrations by
Ben Hodson

ORCA BOOK PUBLISHERS

Jeffrey looked at the blank page. It glared back.

He tried to write but couldn't think of something to write about.

So he doodled instead.

His ideas came slowly, and he found himself sketching a round-bellied, long-armed sloth.

"Just forget about the words," whispered a voice.

Jeffrey looked around, his eyes wide.
"Who said that?"

Down on the page, now covered with doodles, the sloth he had just sketched looked different. "Hey, I didn't draw you with your hands on your hips!" Jeffrey said.

"Good writers have lots of ideas," declared Sloth. "*You* don't have any!"

"Whoa!" Jeffrey jumped to his feet.

"You should stick to drawing," said Sloth.

"W-w-what d-do you know anyway?" Jeffrey stammered.

"I know you're a lousy writer," said Sloth.

"I am not a lousy writer! I just can't think of anything to write about."

"Well, instead of drawing the CN Tower,
make yourself useful and sketch me a chair."
Sloth pointed at a perfect spot on the page.

Jeffrey sat down and did as he was told. He drew an overstuffed chair.

Sloth relaxed into the chair. "This is good, but a pillow would make it even better. Draw me a puffy pillow."

Jeffrey drew a pillow.

"Now sketch me a cozy blanket."

"Urgh," Jeffrey said. "I'll never finish my homework at this rate!"

Sloth laughed. "You're right," he said. "It *is* taking forever. So do something you're good at and draw me a blanket."

Jeffrey was tired of listening to Sloth.
He began to write.

Once there was a pudgy sloth who searched
for the world's coziest blanket.

"Who are you calling pudgy?" Sloth said.
Jeffrey ignored Sloth and went on writing.

He looked up high for that blanket.

Sloth looked to the sky.

He looked down low for that blanket.

Sloth peeked under the chair.

"I sure would like that blanket."

Jeffrey now realized what was happening. "Oh, I get it. You don't want me to write because you're lazy."

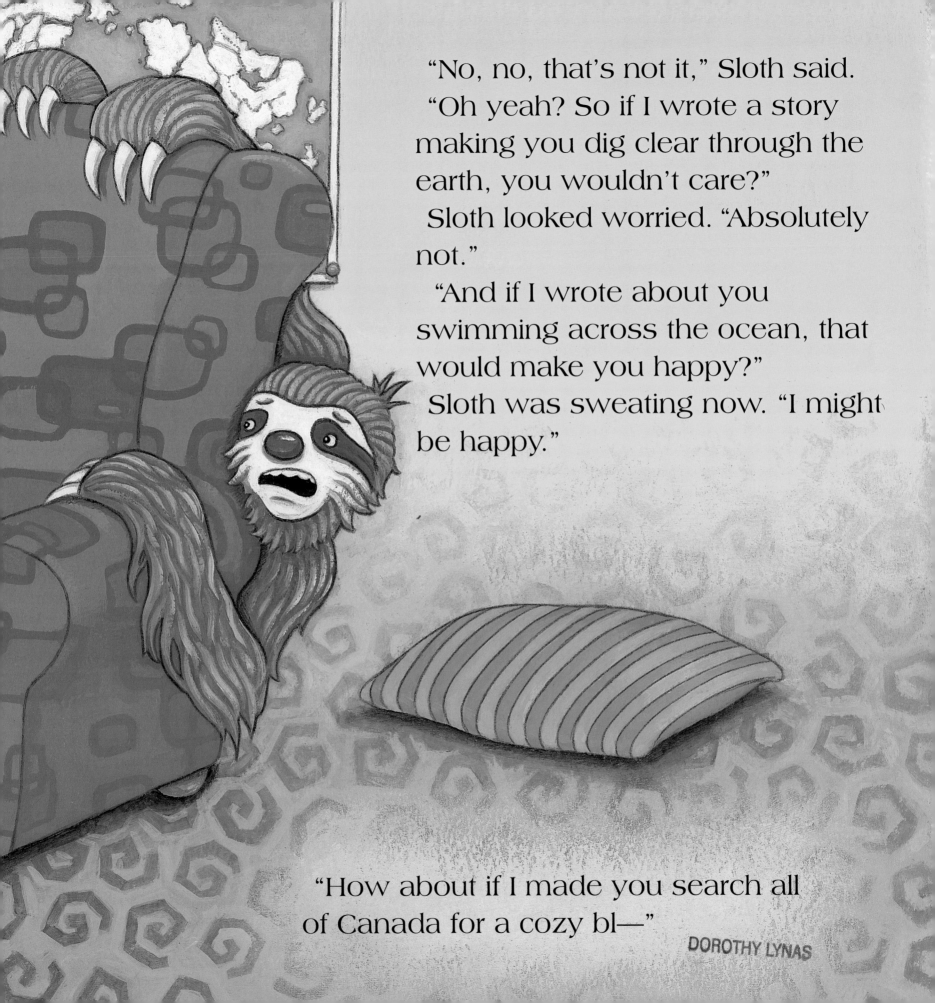

"No, no, that's not it," Sloth said. "Oh yeah? So if I wrote a story making you dig clear through the earth, you wouldn't care?"

Sloth looked worried. "Absolutely not."

"And if I wrote about you swimming across the ocean, that would make you happy?"

Sloth was sweating now. "I might be happy."

"How about if I made you search all of Canada for a cozy bl—"

DOROTHY LYNAS

Sloth interrupted. "If I could find that cozy blanket, I wouldn't mind."

"You realize that Canada is a big place? You would have to climb mountains, trek across the tundra, paddle the Great Lakes and hike the prairies."

"Well, you can't make me!"

"Oh yeah?" Jeffrey said.
He picked up his pencil, sketched a shovel
and continued his story.

He began to dig.

Sloth had no choice but to pick up the shovel and dig.

He dug a hole clear through the earth to India.

"Now I need some water. Quick, write about water," ordered Sloth.

Then he swam to France. He really wanted to find the world's coziest blanket.

"That's not what I meant!
This water is freezing!"
said Sloth, his teeth chattering.

But the coziest blanket wasn't there.

Now Jeffrey was smiling.

"Ahem," Sloth said. His claws dragged on the ground. "I'm afraid that I made a great mistake." Sloth was panting. He was not used to so much exercise. "I said that your writing was lousy," Sloth huffed. "I was wrong. I should have said that your writing is very engaging. And that it makes a lot of sense. Honestly, I mean that. In fact, you're a good...no, a great...no, a marvelous writ—"

"Okay," said Jeffrey.
He looked down at the page.
"Yes!" he cheered. Thanks to Sloth, his
homework was done! Jeffrey beamed
as he sketched a blanket and wrote:

And finally, the very tired sloth found the world's coziest blanket, wrapped himself up in it and fell fast asleep...

at least for that evening.

To my family and friends, for their support and inspiration; and to my
fellow writers, for their inspiration and support. Special thanks to Jonah, David,
Lori, Alison, Theresa, Carl, Sarah, Mary, Loris, Shelley and Maggie. K-L. W.

To my brother, Ted, my kindred spirit in the fine art of daydreaming. B.H.

Library and Archives Canada Cataloguing in Publication

Winters, Kari-Lynn, 1969-

Jeffrey and Sloth / written by Kari-Lynn Winters;
illustrated by Ben Hodson.

ISBN-13: 978-1-55143-323-3   ISBN-10: 1-55143-323-0

I. Hodson, Ben II. Title.

PS8645.I58J43 2007   jC813'.6   C2006-906077-0

Summary: When a doodle tries to take over Jeffrey's life, Jeffrey uses the written word to put it back in its place.

First published in the United States 2007

Library of Congress Control Number: 2006937026

Orca Book Publishers gratefully acknowledges the support for its publishing programs provided by
the following agencies: the Government of Canada through the Book Publishing Industry Development Program
and the Canada Council for the Arts, and the Province of British Columbia through the
BC Arts Council and the Book Publishing Tax Credit.

Orca Book Publishers   **Orca Book Publishers**
PO Box 5626 Stn. B   PO Box 468
Victoria, BC Canada   Custer, WA USA
V8R 6S4   98240-0468

Book design by Doug McCaffry.
Artwork rendered in acrylic and colored pencil on watercolor paper.

Color Separations: ScanLab, Victoria, British Columbia.

Printed and bound in Hong Kong
10 09 08 07 • 4 3 2 1